Balm

For The

heart

Balm for the Heart

E.B. WHEELER

Rowan Ridge
Press

ISBN: 978-1-7360411-8-5

First printing: November 2022

Published by Rowan Ridge Press, Utah

Cover images © Mary Lacy and dariakom

Cover and interior design © Rowan Ridge Press

 Created with Vellum

For the peacemakers

Chapter One

LIZA BALLARD PACED in front of her little army of sorority girls assembled at Bushnell General Military Hospital. It was time for them to do their part for the war effort. Liza inspected the girls to be sure each one passed muster. The girls' hair was curled, the skirts of their floral dresses were full of swing, and they had drawn lines up the back of their legs to imitate the look of the nylon stockings they had given up for the war effort—not a single one smudged.

Liza nodded her approval.

The girls stood at attention beside the bus that had brought them to Brigham City from Utah Agricultural College in Logan with the gas ration provided by the Red Cross. The warm evening air smelled faintly of diesel and freshly baked bread from the hospital kitchens. Spring came a little sooner to Brigham City than Logan. The setting sun painted gold over the orchards, and the breeze blowing from the bird refuge promised summer and—perhaps—an end to the war.

The newspapers claimed that Hitler had been found dead in his bunker. It seemed too good to be true. Liza couldn't see past the dark fog that the war had pulled over everything—couldn't remember clearly what it was like before the war and couldn't imagine what would happen after. In the meantime, Liza would strike against the Germans and their allies in Japan however she could, even if only from the home front.

Liza smiled at the sorority girls, satisfied. "Is everyone ready?"

The girls nodded, some shifting nervously.

"Excellent," Liza said. "Remember, good morale will win the war. That's our mission at these dances—to keep our boys' spirits up."

"Can the men still dance if they're missing a leg?" Carol asked, eyeing the rows of hospital buildings lined up like soldiers for inspection.

Liza smiled at Carol. Her friend was especially shy, and it had been tough to convince her to come to the dance, requiring an appeal to her patriotism.

"Most of them can dance," Liza said, motioning the girls forward. They huddled around her like football players consulting their quarterback. "That's the whole point of Bushnell Hospital. Most of the men have prosthetic limbs, and some have masks that hide facial injuries, but they'll be ready to go back to civilian life soon. We're here to encourage them and let them practice socializing. We don't want them to lose any more to the Germans and Japanese than they already have."

The other Utah Aggie girls listened with interest, and Liza gave them an encouraging smile. She was the expert on dancing with the patients at Bushnell—the soldiers, sailors, and marines—and she liked leading these expeditions. She had been coming down from Cache Valley every month since her parents received the telegram about her brother.

"Well, then how do I look?" Carol adjusted some of her curls and smiled nervously.

Liza laughed. "You look swell. Don't worry. Those boys will be more nervous than you. Some of them haven't even talked to a girl since before the war. Except nurses, I guess."

Carol swatted at a mosquito on her leg, then gasped. "Oh, no! Did I smudge my lines?"

She twisted her leg for inspection.

Someone wolf-whistled, and the group of young women turned to see a blond man with a "PW" on his jumpsuit grinning at them.

"*Du bist wunderschön!*" the man called. "*Willst du mich heiraten? Bitte?*"

Carol shrank back and looked around at the other young people milling on the hospital road, her eyes wide with panic. "There are Germans here? Real Nazis? Why?"

Liza put a reassuring hand on Carol's arm. "He's a prisoner of war. The well-behaved ones are allowed out to work—to earn their keep. Like the work camp they're building at the fairgrounds in Logan. After all, why should they sit around like they're on vacation while our boys fight over there?"

3

She gave the POW a warning glare, and he chuckled and went back to his wheelbarrow.

"That's one of the well-behaved ones, huh?" another girl asked, a bitter edge to her voice.

As the Allies pushed their way into Germany, the folks at home learned the realities of how the Germans treated American POWs. The *North Cache News* had even run a large picture of one of the liberated American POWs, hardly more than a living skeleton. Liza had stared in horror at the image, then torn the newspaper to shreds. These cheerful, well-fed German prisoners were a far cry from the starving American boys who had to be carried out of the German camps on stretchers.

"My parents live close to the fairgrounds," a petite brunette said, her voice tight. "I hope they're going to be safe with the work camp there."

"The POWs have guards," Liza reminded her, though she was glad she lived in Smithfield, far enough north that she wouldn't need to have anything to do with the Germans. "Besides, Hitler is supposed to be dead, remember? The Germans know they're almost beat. We'll crush them and then take care of Japan."

Liza led the way into the hospital. The tan brick buildings were connected by enclosed ramps providing protection from the bitter northern Utah winters. The girls went inside through the Red Cross building near the center of the complex. Red, white, and blue ribbons festooned the sterile white walls, and big band music pumped down the halls from the auditorium where the band was warming up.

Liza wrinkled her nose. No matter how they decorated

Bushnell, it still smelled like a hospital, with harsh antiseptics failing to mask the stench of wounds and infections. There was a certain dreariness to the long halls and the lines of uniform windows that spoke not only of a hospital, but a military one. The men wore standard issue hospital shirts and pants instead of uniforms, but the "USA MD" on each shirt reminded everyone that Uncle Sam was in charge here. Despite the bleakness of it, Liza ached with the longing that her brother George could have made it to Bushnell.

Though Liza came to the hospital dances each month to help cheer the recovering men, Bushnell always took her by surprise. As the girls marched down the halls, the men laughed and jostled each other, racing wheelchairs down the enclosed ramps and playing catch with someone's prosthetic hand. Maybe it was the excitement of the dance, but there was a camaraderie in those halls that lifted Liza's leaden spirits. Even though every one of the patients in the halls was missing a leg or an arm. Sometimes more than that. Every one of them. It turned Liza's stomach to see the price of the war. The price the world paid for the Japanese and the Germans' pride and aggression.

Thinking of the enemy made something sour bubble inside her, but she pushed it down. She was there to help the men and the war effort. To make certain the enemy's brutal triumph over these wounded soldiers was only temporary. She plastered on a smile and took Carol's arm for the walk into the auditorium.

The dances at Bushnell weren't much different from anywhere else. The men loitered around the edges of the room, some cocky, but most shy. They'd spent time styling their hair and putting on their best polish, though they still wore hospital uniforms. And under the shine of their crisp army-issued clothes, they all wore false limbs: metal and resin arms and legs to replace what the Japanese and the Germans had taken.

Joe McQueen's jazz band had come in from Ogden's notorious 25th Street, trumpets swinging and the drum beating an alluring rhythm. McQueen had been deferred from the war because of his music, and Bushnell was the only place he played for free, entertaining the patients. It was a rare chance for some real fun, and it was hard for Liza to stay down when the fast rhythm of the drums swirled through her chest and made her heart beat faster.

The first patients who found the courage to ask for a dance guided their partners onto the dance floor, the girls' skirts twirling. One man even lifted his partner into the air. The onlookers hooted and clapped, those with only one hand pounding on their thighs or the tables.

Carol flushed and leaned closer to Liza. "Oh, I can't dance like that. Will they expect me to know how?"

Liza bit her lip. Joe McQueen's band wouldn't be playing any waltzes or polkas. Liza itched to get out on the floor and swing to the music, but Carol looked terrified as she watched the dancers.

Liza took her arm. "How about we go talk with some of those men in the wheelchairs? They won't be dancing tonight, and I bet they'd like some company, too."

Carol's eyes lit up, and she nodded. Liza walked with her friend over to the men in wheelchairs. A couple of ambulatory Black and Asian patients lingered on the edges of the room with them—not segregated in the hospital but probably not sure if dancing with the white girls was a safe idea, even at Bushnell.

"How are you fellows tonight?" Liza asked.

The men smiled and spilled out a variety of cheerful answers.

One of the men offered Carol and Liza Coca-Colas, a luxury outside the military hospital.

Liza held her bottle out, and another soldier opened the top.

She took a sip. Cold and fizzy and so sweet after rationing sugar. She smiled. "Is it true they serve these on the front?"

"Yes, ma'am," one soldier said. "The Coca-Cola Colonels kept us well supplied."

They all laughed, and Carol joined in. Liza smiled and gave her friend an encouraging look.

"Where do you men call home?" Carol asked quietly.

Bushnell was the hospital for soldiers, sailors, and marines from the West Coast. Some had served in Europe and even more in the Pacific. All the patients, so close to being home, were excited to talk about where they came from and what they looked forward to most when they left. They blurted out a wave of responses.

"Hawaii. I can't wait to eat fresh pineapple again."

"California."

"My wife and little girl are waiting for me in Washington."

"Liza?" a man's voice broke through the noise. "Liza Ballard?"

Liza gave a start and turned to see Jack Jensen staring at

her. His brown hair was trimmed in a short military haircut, and he was thinner than she remembered, but there was no mistaking her brother's best friend. Her heart fluttered as it always had at his grin, but then a wave of unreality swept over her. Jack should not be there. Not without George.

Jack seemed to sense it, too. He paled and quickly looked away.

With a gesture at the soldier next to him, Jack said, "Uh, Liza, this is Robert Decker. Robert, this is Liza Ballard. George's little sister," he added quietly.

She flinched like he'd knocked the air out of her. Was that who she still was? George's little sister? What did that mean now that George was gone? Seeing Jack had made Liza think her brother might be just out of sight. The two had been inseparable. Now, the war had finally, decisively separated them. Liza's eyes stung, but she could not cry there, not in front of these men who had given so much.

That thought made her look more closely at her brother's best friend. Jack, star of the high school baseball team, now sported a prosthetic arm ending in a metal hook—or rather, two metal hooks that opened and closed like a pair of needle-nose pliers—in place of a right hand. Another thing the Germans had stolen. Cold anger smothered the more tender emotions beneath her tears.

Jack cleared his throat. "Liza, Robert served in Germany. With me. And George."

Liza tried to keep her expression pleasant, though she suddenly wanted to run from the hot room with its too-loud music and cheerful crowds. "It's a pleasure to meet you." She hesitated. She desperately wanted to ask about George, but this was not the time. "How long have you been at Bushnell?"

Jack and Robert exchanged a look.

"I was wounded in January," Jack said. "Robert?"

"Right after Christmas, during the Battle of the Bulge." Robert raised his pant leg a little to show off a prosthetic leg. "This was my New Year's gift from the Nazis."

Jack chuckled. "I guess my new hand was supposed to be for Valentine's Day? What a bunch of sweethearts." He caught a glimpse of Liza's expression and sobered a little. "Sorry. Gallows humor." And then he winced again. "I... I'm sorry, Liza. About George."

Liza nodded, not trusting herself to speak.

The band shifted to a softer tone, and the three of them stood there awkwardly, on the edge of saying things that were too serious for a fun night of dancing, but feeling a little too heavy to join in the merriment.

Both men said at the same time, "Do you want to dance?"

Jack and Robert laughed at each other. Liza was glad they weren't watching the blush creep across her face. When she and Jack had been in high school together, she would have loved a dance with him, but now it just seemed uncomfortable.

"I'll fight you for her," Jack joked, brandishing his prosthetic hook at Robert.

"Ah, you know I need to practice dancing on this leg of mine," Robert said.

Jack made a gesture of surrender. "Okay, you win, friend." He grinned at Liza, though it looked strained. "Maybe next time, eh?"

She smiled and nodded stiffly. Carol was doing fine talking with the men in the wheelchairs, so Liza allowed Robert to take her to the dance floor. She resisted the impulse to look back at Jack. She wasn't there for herself. She was there to help the other American boys since there was nothing left she could do for George.

Chapter Two

Jack retreated from the auditorium, the screams of the trumpets and saxophones chasing him into the hall. He would never adjust to post-war life. Like asking Liza to dance. What had he been thinking? He shook his head. He usually didn't come to the dances. It was hard to do anything that felt normal, especially when George should have been there, too. And of course, the one time he did show up, Liza Ballard had to be there. He'd had an impulse to be close to her. Maybe because it felt like a connection to that old life that was gone now.

That wasn't fair to Liza, though. She probably resented him for coming home without George. Then he put her in that awkward situation, making her feel obligated to dance with him. He didn't want any girl to think she had to dance with him, and he didn't want to make things harder on Liza. He'd been around their house all the time when they were younger, and now she'd lost her brother. And here Jack was, alive but still figuring out his new hand, and expecting—what? Not pity. He did not want pity.

Jack leaned his head back against the wall, swatting some bunting out of the way. The music echoed in the hall and hummed in his skull, making his head itch. He raised his right arm to scratch it, then stared at his hook. He still forgot sometimes. Old habits outlasted the limbs they were attached to. If only the doctors could have saved his arm. Then he could have gone back to Germany or even to the Pacific and helped finish the fight.

"Is everything all right, corporal?" a voice asked behind him.

Jack turned to see one of his physical therapists watching him, a knowing sympathy in his eyes.

"Yes, sir," Jack said, reminding himself that he didn't salute his therapist. "I just needed some fresh air."

"Understandable," the therapist said. He glanced back into the auditorium. "You're ready for this, corporal. Give yourself a chance."

"Thank you, sir," Jack said.

The physical therapist stood there waiting, not giving Jack a chance to keep lingering in the hall.

Jack peeked into the auditorium and caught a glimpse of Liza dancing with Robert. She looked so... grown up. It was probably because she wore her brunette hair in curls and was wearing a nice dress. And lipstick, maybe? He'd glanced at her lips but tried not to stare. She'd always been the girl in the overalls and braids working alongside the guys. Tonight, she was definitely not one of the guys.

But she was still George's little sister. The hollow ache

rose in his chest the same as it always did when he thought of George. It was just a matter of bad luck, he told himself again and again, a matter of who was standing where when the attack came. But that didn't bring George back, and it didn't make Jack feel any better that he was there in Utah, almost home again, while George was never coming back.

He slipped back into the auditorium and reached for a Coca-Cola bottle with his hook. He focused on keeping the hook at the best angle. The strap that opened and closed the two sides of the hook ran across his opposite shoulder, and the muscle movements that controlled how far it opened were almost natural by now. He grasped the bottle and picked it up. An accomplishment, but not as satisfying as feeling the cool glass against his palm.

Jack switched the bottle to his left hand and took a sip, hardly tasting the sweetness as he watched the dancers. His gaze fell on Liza and Robert again, but he quickly looked elsewhere. Amputees packed the auditorium, talking to the girls and testing out their coordination with their limbs.

"You look worried," said a voice at his elbow.

Jack looked over to see his cousin Albert Lewis in a wheelchair, watching the dancing. Albert had needed another surgery on his amputated leg, so he wasn't walking yet, even though he'd arrived at Bushnell before Jack. The place was like a grim class reunion. Jack couldn't think of any friends or family who hadn't been affected by the war.

Jack sat. "I'm just wondering what's going to happen to all of us when we go back to civilian life."

Albert nodded. "It won't be as easy as it is here." He

grinned. "I'm still working my way up to that free meal at the Idle Isle."

Jack chuckled. Brigham City was good to the wounded men. The owners of the Idle Isle cafe gave them a free meal the first time they could walk through the front door unassisted. But Jack had grown up on a farm. He'd learned that the rest of the world didn't slow down and watch out for you. You had to keep up.

He studied his prosthetic hook. He had a prosthetic arm that appeared real, if you didn't look too closely. But he always wore his hook. It was practical—could get things done —though it had taken months of practice to get to that point. Without it, he felt naked. Helpless. He wasn't a full person without it. Even as it was, he wasn't sure he'd really be able to lead a normal life.

The band started up the fast rhythm of "Caravan." Jack used to like the song, but now, it grated on his spine. He glanced back into the hall. No sign of the lurking therapist. He rose to his feet.

"Hey, Jack," Albert said.

Jack looked back, feeling like he'd been caught going AWOL.

"It won't be the same, but that doesn't mean it won't be good." Albert raised his Coca-Cola and took a swig.

Jack forced a smile and retreated to the relative quiet of the halls. Bushnell had started to feel as much like home as anywhere else. It was hard to believe he'd soon leave behind the dreary halls, bland food, and constant physical therapy— and the companionship of other men who understood. A flare of panic rose in his chest, hot and sputtering, but he squelched it and kept walking.

After the band packed away their instruments and the girls went home, Robert caught up with Jack wandering the enclosed ramps connecting the buildings.

"Hey!" Robert called, limping to catch up with Jack. "I'm surprised you didn't stay for every song."

"Why's that?"

"This is probably your last dance, isn't it? Aren't they sending you home soon?"

Jack glanced down at his hook. "Yeah. I suppose it was my last dance."

"Don't worry," Robert said. "We'll be heroes at home. Lots of girls to dance with there, too."

"Yeah, sure," Jack said.

He thought the shine of heroism would probably fade, and with it the girls anxious to dance with a crippled soldier. America would celebrate the end of the war when they finally beat Germany and Japan—celebrate the men coming home—and then move on. The soldiers would be expected to move on, too.

"George's little sister is a looker, isn't she?" Robert asked.

"Well, I suppose she is."

"Spunky, though. She'll be a handful for some poor, lucky chap."

Jack's hackles rose, and he turned on Robert. "Hey, that's George's sister you're talking about."

"Right, sorry." Robert didn't look sorry. His train of thought seemed to have already moved elsewhere. Probably to a different girl.

Jack shook his head.

Ahead of them, a German POW mopped the floor, gazing wistfully toward the empty auditorium. Jack's heart went out to the fellow. Any POWs allowed to come to the camps in Utah had already been screened carefully to ensure that they were not a danger to the community—that they had no loyalty to the Nazi party. Most of them had been forced to fight and were glad enough to be out of it. They knew little if any English, but they couldn't have missed the news that Germany's defense was collapsing. The German POWs seemed anxious, no doubt worrying about their families back home, about to be overrun by occupying armies. The Americans, Jack thought, would treat the Germans well enough, but the Russians were out for revenge.

The POW leaned on his mop and eyed Jack and Robert's hospital uniforms enviously.

Jack wished he could say something comforting to the POW. His mother was Swiss and knew German, but she'd stopped speaking it during the First World War, so it became a part of Jack's heritage that he couldn't connect to.

He held up his half-finished Coca-Cola and said, *"Bitte?"* It seemed to be the word Germans used for everything polite.

"Ja?" The German eyed the bottle with a mix of longing and skepticism.

Jack smiled and held the bottle out, and the German took it with an answering grin.

"Coca-Cola!" he said with a heavy accent, and he laughed at himself along with Jack and Robert. *"Danke, danke!"*

"Enjoy it, friend," Jack said.

The German sipped the drink like it was ambrosia. Jack imagined he hadn't had a treat for a long time, and if he was going to be sent back to Germany when the war was over, he wouldn't have a treat again for an even longer time. As hard as things were for the Americans returning home, Jack did not envy the German POWs.

"Careful there," Robert said. "People are going to think you're fraternizing with the enemy."

Robert's grin showed he was teasing, but Jack only managed a weak chuckle in return. Most people probably wouldn't understand his sympathy for the German soldiers. Most civilians wouldn't, anyway. Jack felt like he had more in common with the POWs than with someone like Liza Ballard. He groaned inwardly. No matter what the doctors and therapists said, he was far from ready for civilian life.

Chapter Three

"THIS CANNOT POSSIBLY BE good for morale," Liza muttered.

She stood on her front porch, a light drizzle of cool June rain making a curtain off the eaves and filling the air with the scent of wet earth. Soon, the convoy of German prisoners of war would pass by. Regardless of what Liza and her neighbors thought of it, the army had completed the Logan prisoner of war camp. Now, every day, a convoy of trucks carried the Germans from their camp at the Logan Fairgrounds to the local fields across Cache Valley to weed sugar beets. With so many men gone to fight, the farms needed the extra help, but it gave Liza a chill to see all those German men rolling by, as if her community were being invaded.

And then the rumors had started. Things were going missing around town. Mrs. Price swore some of her sugar ration coupons had vanished from her purse. A local store reported that someone had robbed a display of Kodak cameras. It probably had nothing to do with the POWs, but Liza didn't remember such things happening before the war, and the guards watching the POWs didn't pay close attention.

Liza couldn't do anything about it, but every morning she watched the Germans go by, as if she could somehow deter them from hurting anyone. People had hoped that if they treated the German POWs well, then the Germans would treat the Americans well, but they knew now that had been a false hope. As if anything were fair in war. And the Germans, it seemed, were monsters in human form.

The rumble of the trucks' wheels over the road caught her ear. A dozen vehicles rolled down the road, each with a local farmer in the driver's seat and an armed American soldier seated beside him. The Germans in the back laughed together and gabbed as though weeding beet fields in the drizzle was a treat. Liza frowned and wrapped her arms around her middle. George should have been there, working in his own family's fields, instead of these German strangers.

One of the trucks slowed. The driver was Alonzo Jensen —Jack's father. He waved, and Liza returned the gesture.

"How are you this morning, Liza?" he asked. "Planning something for us for the Fourth of July?"

"Of course," she said. "A war bond carnival."

He chuckled. "It's sure great how you've stepped up. George would be proud."

Liza just nodded. She couldn't stop and think about George. She just kept moving or she would sink into a despair she didn't know how to climb out of.

"We're bringing Jack home soon," Mr. Jensen said. "I bet he'd love to help with the carnival."

"That would be swell," Liza said, though she wasn't sure. Without George around, who was Jack to her?

The trucks drove on to the farms, planted thick with sugar beets for the war effort. Liza was about to go back in the house when she heard a commotion. She turned and shielded her eyes against the sun breaking through the clouds. Some of the neighborhood boys, led by the local pre-teen troublemaker Wayne Vaughn, rode their bikes alongside the trucks, yelling and throwing rocks at the Germans.

Liza rolled her eyes and jogged out into the drizzle to catch up with the trucks, which slowed to a stop.

The rear driver got out, along with the guard, who showed little interest in defending his charges against a pack of boys.

"You boys knock it off or I'll tan your hides!" the driver shouted at the kids, looking like he meant it.

"We're just fighting the Nazis!" Wayne yelled back.

He glared at the men in the truck, who returned his stare with various degrees of sullenness or defiance.

The guard smirked.

Liza grabbed Wayne's arm as he prepared to hurl another missile. "Stop it!"

Wayne released the rock and jerked away from her grip. "I hate the Nazis!" His face was red with anger, but tears shimmered in his eyes. "They killed my brother!"

And with that, his defiance dissolved, and he started bawling. Liza wrapped the boy in an embrace. She hadn't heard about the Vaughn's son, but there were so many men killed, she didn't have the heart to scan the papers anymore for names. After all, her worst fears had been realized. There were no more names for her to search for on that list.

"I'm sorry," Liza whispered.

The German POWs looked away, embarrassed for Wayne or perhaps understanding somewhat his anger.

"I want Billy back!" Wayne sobbed into Liza's shoulder.

Her eyes prickled with sympathetic tears, and she held him closer. "I know, I know."

When Wayne's sobs abated somewhat, she pulled back from him. "Do you know why we can't harm the prisoners of war?"

He wiped his eyes on his sleeve and shook his head, his hair damp from the rain.

"There are rules for everything, even for war. It's against the rules to hurt the people who have surrendered."

"They're the bad guys," Wayne said.

"Yes, they are. But we have to be the good guys. Do you understand?"

"I guess." Wayne picked up his dog's leash and got back on his bike.

Liza watched him go, a heaviness settling in her stomach. Once she was alone on the street, she picked up a rock and hurled it after the trucks. It bounced harmlessly—futilely—on the road.

She made it back into the house before her own tears came.

Chapter Four

CACHE VALLEY. The sight of the Bear River meandering through green fields, all sheltered by the mountains, relieved some of the tension in Jack's shoulders. With everything else that had changed, the valley didn't look so different from when he had left it. Fields of dairy cows watched his father's truck roll past, and Jack stared back at them, even enjoying—a little—the familiar scent of cattle.

He was home. He glanced at the empty seat beside him where George should have been.

Sort of.

It had been odd recovering at Bushnell, so close to home that his family came to visit often, but still not in Cache Valley where he would have to face the past and the future. After traveling overseas, fighting, and being wounded, the valley seemed smaller than he remembered, but that just made it more snug, its peace like a blanket he could wrap himself in and—hopefully—finally rest.

Of course, he hadn't expected the valley to be the same as before the war. Too many people were gone. Especially George. They'd done everything together: played baseball, graduated North Cache High School, studied at Utah Agricultural College, enlisted for the army. The only thing they hadn't done together was come home.

Now, Jack wasn't even sure who he was anymore. What would people expect of him? He had to act brave; he knew that. He had to deny the quivering fear of the future—of being weak or a failure—that had lodged in his belly.

Jack sighed and leaned his head against the cool glass of the window. He had learned to repair cars at Bushnell with his prosthetic hook, and they had tried to help him be prepared for civilian life, but how could they? Cache Valley hadn't changed much, but he had, and he didn't know what kind of life he could expect to have.

When they drove past George's house, the pain almost crumpled Jack. He closed his eyes, but not before glimpsing Liza watching from the front window.

As the car rumbled on, that glance of Liza lingered in his imagination. It might be nice to talk to her. She was the other person who knew George best. But it would also be strange, just the two of them without George there to fill in the silences.

At least the Jensen family farm wasn't silent. His dad pulled the truck up in front of the old family home.

Jack's mother Trudi rushed out to embrace him. She had more streaks of gray in her hair than he remembered, but her familiar scent of fresh baked bread and roasted apples made him feel for a moment as though he had never left.

"I'm so glad you're home," she whispered in his ear.

Jack's younger siblings approached more slowly—almost shyly. They had come to see him once in the hospital after he'd recovered enough that his injuries wouldn't frighten them, and they had been wide-eyed and somber then. But now, he was really among them again. He hugged each of them in turn and commented on how much they'd grown. Their height really did surprise him. His youngest sister, Sarah, had only been five when he left, and now she was seven. His brother, Leroy, was as tall as him now. His name would be in the draft soon. Jack hoped it never came to that. Wasn't that why he and George had gone to fight? To stop evil before it reached their homes?

"You playing baseball this summer?" he asked Leroy.

"A little. I'm not as good at pitching as you are." His brother flushed and glanced at his prosthetic. "Uh, were."

Jack refused to be shaken by that reminder. "Well, we'll have to practice, then. You'll be better than me in no time."

The ice broken, his younger sisters stepped forward to chatter about their activities: piano and singing in church plays and knitting for the Red Cross. None of them said anything about his prosthetic, but they all stole glances, their expressions troubled, even a little afraid. Jack couldn't bear that. He didn't want his family shy of him.

He held up his prosthetic hook, and it drew their attention, bringing the conversation to a stuttering halt. The youngest girls stared openly.

Jack grinned and bent toward the girls. "Arrr! Which of you is the crocodile that ate me hand? I blame that wretched Peter Pan!"

The younger girls squealed in delight as Jack chased them, clicking the two parts of the hook open and closed. He caught Sarah and swung her over his shoulder with his good arm. "I've caught Tinker Bell!"

Sarah's sisters came to her rescue, pounding on Jack.

"I'm not Tinker Bell!" Sarah said between giggle fits. "I'm Sarah!"

"Oh, sorry, miss. You little fairies all look the same."

He returned the laughing girl to her sisters, and they ran off babbling about Peter Pan.

"They were supposed to shell peas," his mother said, hands on her hips.

"Sorry, Ma," he said in mock chagrin.

She wrapped him in a tight embrace and whispered, "I'm just so glad you're here."

He squeezed her back. "Me too."

Out in the fields, where normally Jack would be working, a row of men in shirts labeled PW bent over the sugar beets. Jack's father caught the direction of his stare and put an arm on his shoulder.

"I hope they don't upset you."

"Who? The Germans? No, we had some at Bushnell, too. They're just soldiers who were on the wrong side."

Leroy looked surprised by that, but seemed still too shy of his older brother to question him.

Their father nodded. "I've always hated how war turns people into enemies. Happened in the last war, too. Your mother had a rough time, even though she's not actually German..." He cleared his throat. "These fellows don't seem like bad men. Of course, I don't understand a thing they're saying."

Jack chuckled. "Might be better for the women's ears that way." Though, his mother still understood German, even if she refused to speak it. "Do they work hard?"

"Hard enough. I think they'd rather be here than locked up in some camp with nothing to do. Your mother makes them a big lunch like she would with any other field hands, so they eat well, at least. Last year, we had workers from the Japanese camp down at Topaz."

"Japanese POWs?"

"No, a lot of them were Americans, rounded up from the coast to be sure they weren't spies. They all spoke English. Told us about the camps and how glad they were to have something to do. It doesn't sit right with me, though, thinking of America-born men—and women and children!—put into camps. At least these POWs are better off than where they were before."

Jack nodded. How often he had wished he could be on the farm instead of on the battlefield. But that was when he was dreaming of his own farm, not someone else's. Still, when his mother brought out drinks for the men, they did look pretty content being where they were.

"Jack!"

His older sister, Rose, walked over, carrying a blonde-haired toddler on one hip.

"Rose!" He rushed to embrace his sister, and the toddler shied away from him.

"Gladys, darling," Rose said. "No need to be shy. This is your Uncle Jack!"

Jack swept the girl an exaggeratedly gallant bow, and she smiled a little before hiding her face in her mother's shoulder again.

"Okay, go play, Gladys." Rose set the girl down, and she immediately toddled for their parents' long-suffering collie.

Some of the Germans sipping their lemonade watched absentmindedly as the girl patted the dog. One of the men, however, set down his glass and took a few steps forward, his stare riveted on the toddler. He said something excitedly to his comrades in German and walked closer to the oblivious child.

Rose frowned and stepped nearer to her daughter. The armed guard, who up to this point had been barely paying attention, reached for his gun.

The German POW stopped and tore his gaze from Gladys to look at Rose, then back at the child. His eyes filled with tears.

"*Und wo ist mein Kind jetzt?*" he said.

He crumpled to the ground, wrapped his arms around his knees, and watched the little girl with tears streaming down his cheeks. The other Germans put down their glasses, some of them turning away to hide their faces from the scene, others watching with watery eyes.

"What's happening?" Rose asked.

"I think they're worried about their families," Jack whispered.

His mother's eye brimmed with tears. "Yes. He has a little girl like Gladys, but he doesn't know where she is now."

Rose looked startled, as if it hadn't occurred to her that these men left mothers and wives, siblings and children behind. It was odd to Jack to think of families behind the front, to remember that the people he had shot at and who had shot at him had loved ones waiting for them. He couldn't think of that out there, but here, it crashed down on him.

He pulled out a clean, white handkerchief and walked across the field to hand it to the enemy soldier sitting on the ground on his parents' farm. He felt his family's curious and startled stares, and the wary watch of the guard, but he couldn't look away from the suffering German. The man noted Jack's prosthetic and met his eyes. Then, he reached out and took the white cloth, clutching it tightly. Jack nodded once, and the man returned the gesture, a silent truce of understanding between them.

Chapter Five

Liza turned a soft lump of risen dough out onto the counter, a little cloud of flour puffing around her. She winced, not wanting to waste any of it. She and her mother had learned to make a simple, long-rising bread without sugar or oil, using just a little slice of their cake of fresh yeast to stretch their ration stamps as far as possible. Every time she saw an ingredient wasted, Liza thought of the empty spots on the grocery store shelves and felt a flutter of panic.

Someone knocked on the front door. Liza's mother was out in the garden, taking scraps to the chickens, and her father was working in town, so Liza wiped her hands on her apron and hurried out to answer it.

Jack stood on her front porch, wearing a civilian suit with his hat in his hands. Or rather, one hand and one hook. He hadn't knocked before, when George was still alive.

"Uh, hello," Jack said. "My dad said you were planning

something for the Fourth of July. To encourage people to buy war bonds. I wanted to see if there was something I could do to help. Anything to see the end of this war."

"Oh." Liza hadn't expected this. Jack had never paid much attention to what Liza did before. She admired him for not giving up the fight, though. "That would be swell. Come in. I was making bread, but it's almost ready for its second rise."

Jack nodded, fidgeting with his hat and looking around the room, his forehead creased. Liza left him in the parlor and hurried back to shape the loaves. Before she returned from the kitchen, she took a moment to hang her apron up and straighten her hair. Not that it mattered what she looked like. It was only Jack.

He stood waiting in the front parlor, his eyes tracing everything in the room, probably taking in the little changes. The last pictures of George in his uniform. The telegram. The service flag with its gold star. Finally, he looked up to meet her gaze.

"Please, sit down," she said. How odd, to be so formal with someone who once practically lived in their house. "What did you have in mind? For helping?"

"Oh, I don't know. If George were here—"

He stopped and stared at the gold star. Liza didn't interrupt his thoughts. She couldn't stand to look at the gold star, but maybe Jack still needed to get used to it. Finally, he looked at her again, his eyes glistening a little.

"I'm not sure," Jack said. "I don't really know anymore..."

Liza stepped in. That was what she had grown used to: organizing, staying busy, staying focused.

She gestured to the piles of red, white, and blue crepe paper and threadbare donated fabric. "We need decorations. A lot of them. You could help tie the ribbons..." she glanced at his prosthetic and her face warmed. "Er, I mean, if you can."

He smiled ruefully and picked up a long strip of ribbon reclaimed from a worn out dress someone had given to the cause. In a few moments, he had tied a passable bow, using his hook to pull it tight.

"That's wonderful," Liza said.

"Because I only have one good hand?" He didn't look offended.

She smiled. "Actually, because it's the best bow I've ever seen a man tie."

He chuckled. "They made us practice at Bushnell. They wanted us to leave with practical skills."

"In case you wanted to work as a bow maker?"

"Isn't it a popular job?" He grinned, showing off a single dimple and bright blue eyes, and something in her chest fluttered. "I also learned to repair engines."

"Normally, that would be the more useful skill, but the bows are what we need for the carnival."

"Great!" He picked up a strip of crepe paper, careful not to tear it with his hook.

Liza had seen enough of the men at Bushnell to know they could take care of themselves, but she was impressed with Jack's dexterity with his prosthetic. Her bread was still rising, and she didn't like to be idle, so she picked up a strip of crepe paper, too. She went to work on her bow, glancing occasionally at Jack. He finished first, but she thought hers was a little fluffier. Jack grabbed another piece of crepe, and

Liza hurried to get one, too, trying to keep up. Drat. Jack was fast. She finished her next bow at the same time he did, but this time, hers didn't look as nice as the first one.

She pursed her lips and snatched up another piece of crepe from the pile. Her hand bumped Jack's, and an electric jolt shot straight to her heart. She pretended not to have noticed, but when she looked up from her bow, Jack was grinning at her.

"What?" she asked a little too sharply.

"You're racing me, aren't you?"

She laughed. "Guilty."

"Were you always this competitive?"

She chewed her lip. Was she? Life before the war seemed so long ago. "I suppose I was just looking for an outlet for my fighting spirit."

"And you found it in the glorious old profession of bow making?"

She flipped her hair back. "I have it on good authority that it's a popular profession."

Jack laughed, and she joined him.

A sound from the kitchen doorway made them both look up. Liza's mother stood there, her eyes luminous with tears.

"Mother?" Liza stood quickly.

"I'm fine," her mother said. "It's just been a long time since I heard young people laughing in this house."

She managed a smile, but Liza felt the weight of George's loss settle over the room once again. With her mother back to oversee the bread, Liza continued making bows with Jack, but they mostly worked in silence. Even with the awkwardness of

George hanging between them, the work went much faster with two people.

The front door swung open. Jack looked up, his expression hopeful, as though he expected to see George walk in, as Liza often did. But it was her father returning from work.

"Oh, hello, Jack," Mr. Ballard said. "Found a new way to help the war effort, I see."

"Yes, sir," Jack said with a rueful smile.

"How was your day, Daddy?" Liza asked.

He took off his hat and scratched his thinning hair. "Bit of a ruckus. A house over near the fairgrounds was robbed, and everyone's talking about it."

Heat prickled over Liza's skin. "The Germans!"

"Most likely," her father said.

Jack's mouth tightened, but he didn't say anything.

"Will you stay for dinner, Jack?" Mrs. Ballard asked.

He glanced briefly at Liza, and she thought a question flashed in his eyes, but then he shook his head. "Mother will expect me home."

"Thank you for your help," Liza said as he headed for the door.

He nodded and left, murmuring goodbye.

"Poor young man," her mother said.

Liza glanced at her mother. Did she think his missing hand slowed him down?

But her mother added, "I've never seen a young person looking so lost."

Liza frowned down at the bow in her lap. She felt lost,

too, and when she stopped to think for any amount of time, the anger and grief almost overwhelmed her. So, she couldn't allow herself time to think. She couldn't allow herself distractions—reminders of George. Like Jack.

Chapter Six

Jack took his time walking home from the Ballard's. He'd wanted to point out that the Germans were always under guard and unlikely to risk the consequences of stealing from a nearby house, but he didn't want to start an argument. It had been strange at first to sit in the parlor without George, but he had spent so much time there over the years, it didn't take long for him to start to feel at home again, and he hadn't wanted to disturb that feeling.

He shouldn't let himself get comfortable there, though. With George gone, it was probably awkward for the Ballards to have him around. He didn't really belong there anymore. Liza hadn't seemed to mind the company, at least. He felt like he'd always known her, yet hadn't known her at all. Had the war changed her, too, or had he just not paid attention in the past? He'd wanted to talk to her more, understand her better, but she might feel like he was prying.

He wanted to pry a little. He'd wanted to touch her hand

again, to feel the warmth of her skin. He shook his head. What was he thinking? This was George's little sister. George would probably have dunked him in the irrigation canal for even thinking such a thing.

Jack found his dad in the driveway of their farmhouse with the family's Ford Model 50 pickup truck. His dad had the hood up and muttered some choice words that he would never have said in front of the women of the house.

"Problems with the truck?" Jack asked.

"I'll say! And I have to take the POWs back to their camp." His dad motioned over his shoulder to where the POWs were milling about, chatting with each other in German and looking in no hurry to get back to Logan. "Too bad your Aunt Clara isn't here. She was always good with these old Fords."

"Want me to take a look, sir?" Jack inched closer to the truck. A nice flathead V8 engine. Jack had only paid attention to driving the car before the war, but this was what Bushnell had trained him to do.

His dad looked skeptical, though, and he glanced at Jack's hook. A hot feeling crept up Jack's neck—embarrassment and frustration. Shame. Sure, Jack could tie a pretty bow for Liza, but his dad didn't think he could fix a truck.

"I worked on engines just like this one at Bushnell," Jack said, trying not to sound bitter.

His dad's face softened. "I forgot. Go right ahead."

Jack nodded and dove into the engine. It didn't take him long to spot the problem. "You've got a bad seal here. I can replace it for you."

"That's great, son!"

His dad sounded surprised, but Jack tried not to let it get to him. At least he'd proven that he could do something useful. He pulled the tool box out of the back of the truck and rummaged through it. His dad should have had some extra seals in there.

"*Hier*," said a voice at his elbow.

Jack jumped and looked up at the POW standing behind him. The man grinned nervously and pointed at the part.

Embarrassed that he hadn't spotted it himself, Jack picked it up. "Thanks. Uh, *danke*."

The POW grinned. "*Bitte!*" He cleared his throat. "I am mechanic in the army."

"This is no Mercedes," Jack said, not sure how much English the man understood.

The POW wrinkled his forehead, then he smiled. "*Ach, nein!* No Mercedes. Ford is also in *Deutschland*."

"Yeah, I suppose it is." That was odd, Jack thought, soldiers on both sides using Fords. "Thanks again. *Danke*."

The POW nodded, looking hesitant. "I am Hans."

Jack could feel his dad's curious stare, but he smiled. "Good to meet you Hans. I'm Jack."

"Yack," Hans shook his head. "Shack." He laughed. "English is *schwer*."

Jack laughed, too. "I'm sure it is."

Jack returned to the engine and replaced the seal, hand and hook working together. "Start her up. She should run fine now."

His dad fired up the engine, which purred smoothly with the new seal. "Do you want to ride back into town with me?"

"Sure," Jack said.

He took the passenger seat, while the POWs and their guard clambered into the back of the truck.

Once they were driving down Main Street, his dad said, "You probably shouldn't get too friendly with the prisoners. They're not supposed to fraternize. And people around here don't trust the Germans. They'll wonder what your intentions are."

"Intentions? I don't plan to ask them on a date." Jack snapped. He studied his hook and softened his tone. "They're just soldiers. Like me."

Jack glanced at the back of the truck, where the German POWs lounged. The men looked tired but not unhappy. Only the guard stared glumly out over the golden evening. Probably felt like he was missing the excitement overseas. Not much glory in watching over a bunch of men who'd already been beaten, and some of the guards had a reputation of being less-than-stellar soldiers.

They drove down Main Street in silence, Jack trailing his hook out the open window. The warm summer air slipped up his sleeve. Suddenly, his dad slammed on the brakes, and Jack jolted forward, catching himself on the dashboard with his good hand.

A boy on a bike blocked the road. He hurled a mud ball, which splattered on the windshield.

"Nazis!" the boy yelled.

He hopped on his bike and pedaled off.

Jack's dad growled.

"What was that about?" Jack asked.

His dad shook his head and flipped on the windshield

wipers to clear off the mud. "Wayne Vaughn. His brother died in Germany. He's... struggling."

Jack nodded. He was struggling, too, and he had a grown man's perspective on the war.

They drove down past open farmland into Logan. Main Street hadn't changed much, but when they turned west for the fairgrounds, Jack got an unpleasant jolt. Wooden guard towers looked over the canvas tents that housed the POWs, and a hog wire fence surrounded the fairgrounds. The green lawns and trees of Willow Park stood empty, as did the racetrack. The whole neighborhood had a guarded feel.

"Why did they put the camp here?" Jack asked. "It's awfully far from the farms."

"And right in the middle of town," his dad said. "I don't know why. A lot of people weren't happy about it, but I guess they needed someplace they could guard. The Mexican migrant workers camp out in Amalga, but it would be easy for POWs to escape from there. The guards tell me the Germans are always wanting to head up to the mountains."

Jack nodded. "It probably reminds them of home."

Some of the POW workers at Bushnell sneaked to the mountains occasionally and no one made much fuss—they always came back after a few hours of hiking around—but there were a lot more people in Cache Valley, and, it seemed, a lot more POWs.

His dad parked the truck, and the POWs clambered out of the back. The guard walked them to the checkpoint at the front gate, looking bored. The guard by the gate, though, caught Jack's attention. The young man fidgeted with his gun, his finger sometimes inching toward the trigger. He gave the Germans an undisguised look of disgust as they filed past. Maybe he was extra jumpy because of the theft Mr. Ballard had mentioned.

On the open grass between the tents, two groups of POWs played a game of soccer with a slightly deflated basketball. Most of their fellow prisoners cheered as one side scored, but some of the POW spectators booed and yelled at the players.

One of the Jensen's workers shouted something at the other POWs. Some of the soccer spectators shouted back, and the two groups of men walked toward each other. Jack didn't need to understand German to see that the yelling match was not in good fun.

An officer jogged up next to the guards, who were now all alert.

A prisoner with a white band on his arm shoved one of the Jensen's workers. A group of POWs swarmed the prisoner with the white band, and they tumbled into a heap of swinging fists and elbows.

Jack and his father hopped out of the truck.

One of the guards raised his gun and looked at his officer expectantly. "Should I fire, sir?"

Jack's stomach turned cold. He wanted to tell the private to put his gun down, but Jack wasn't in the army anymore. It wasn't his place. Yet the thought of the guard firing into the unarmed men made him clench his fist and step up to the hog wire fence. His father looked angry, too.

The officer gave the private a sour look. "No shooting." He blew a whistle, and the fighting prisoners broke apart, many holding bleeding noses and swollen lips. He looked at the guards. "Separate those men. Get them back to their tents unless they need medical attention."

The POWs didn't even grumble as they marched back to their tents. The sagging ball sat alone in the field.

The officer noticed Jack and his father watching. He shook his head. "Even with you folks working them out in the fields all day, they still have the energy for that. We let them play sports, have a band, take YMCA classes, but the tension is always there."

"What was it about?" Jack asked.

"We have Germans and Austrians in this camp. The Germans call the Austrians traitors—especially when they wear the white armbands for 'Free Austria'— and the Austrians call the Germans Nazis. I don't know who thought it was a good idea to keep them together, but it makes a headache for me."

"At least they don't team up and try to escape," Jack's father joked.

"Why would they?" The officer gestured around. "They have plenty to eat here and nowhere to go out there. They're just biding their time until Japan is defeated, the war is over, and they can go home."

They said goodnight to the officer and walked back to the truck. Jack noticed someone watching from a window across the street, but when he glanced their way, the curtain quickly fell into place. He frowned and slammed the truck door after he climbed in, earning a warning look from his dad.

Jack hunkered down in his seat for the drive home. The officer had things in hand, but what if he hadn't? Would Jack have stood there and watched that guard shoot the same men who worked his father's fields during the day? Certainly, the war would be over soon, but it would leave problems behind. Jack thought he'd left the hostilities in Europe, but he realized now that wasn't the case, and a wave of helplessness washed over him.

"You know, I didn't fight in the last war," his dad said suddenly.

Jack shrugged. "Not as many men did. We weren't in that war very long."

"I got an agricultural deferment. I didn't think the war was our business. I didn't want to add to the bloodshed."

"Oh," Jack said.

He didn't know about back then, but now, people like that were often called cowards. Still, it might take courage not to fight, too. He knew an army medic who was a conscientious objector—he wouldn't fight, but he'd risk his life to help others. There was nothing cowardly in that. And Jack couldn't imagine his strong, hard-working father as a coward either.

"This war is different," his dad went on. "I still don't like the bloodshed, but we have to stop the Axis powers or we'll never have peace again." His dad glanced over. "When I look at you, sometimes I still see you as a kid. I let myself forget that you're a man now. But you are. Especially after going overseas. You sacrificed over there to bring us peace, and I can see you're willing to do more. It's not easy to be a peacemaker, but I want you to know I'm proud of who you're becoming."

Jack shifted uncomfortably. "I'm not entirely sure who that is."

"That's okay. You'll figure it out. You're showing wisdom and compassion with the Germans. That's impressive."

Jack didn't feel wise. He felt confused, like he was feeling his way through a dark room. But it did warm him a little to know his dad was proud. Maybe he was on the right track, at least. He turned again to watch out the window as the dusk brought darkness over the valley and the first raindrops fell.

Chapter Seven

LIZA COULDN'T REMEMBER A COLDER, wetter June. After so many drizzly days, she had created a huge pile of decorations for the Fourth of July war bond drive, tried every recipe in her mother's "How to Bake by the Ration Book," and was going stir crazy.

When Saturday morning dawned bright and dry, she hurried out to weed in the garden. She would be leading another expedition to Bushnell Hospital soon, and as the pile of weeds beside her grew, she let her mind wander to that next trip. She knew it was impossible, but she imagined finding George there, only missing all this time and not actually dead. She yanked at a long vine of bindweed attempting to climb a tomato plant. The roots stayed behind, and she would just be pulling it up again next week, carefully untwining the strangling plant once again from the young tomatoes. Like Bushnell. She went month after month, danced with dozens of young men in uniforms, but it didn't do anything to cure the empty ache inside of her. It all felt hopeless and pointless.

Liza shook her head and yanked up another clump of bindweed. She had to stay busy. If she was still for too long, her mind went into a dangerous whirl of worry, fear, and anger.

A bee buzzed past, hunting out the bright yellow squash blossoms. Liza's mother had taken to battering and frying the blossoms with just a sprinkle of sugar for a treat. There were few treats left these days. The bee zipped past again, its legs coated with pollen. Liza envied the people with beehives. At least they had honey.

She straightened from the garden and stared off after the bee. Honey could make taffy, as could molasses and maybe even maple syrup. It wouldn't be too much longer before people with bees would get a new harvest of honey, and if they had enough left now to donate, taffy would make a fine treat for the boys at Bushnell.

Within a few minutes, Liza had washed up and was on the phone, wheedling a bit of sugar here and some extra honey there from her neighbors, and notifying her army of girls to meet at the church building's kitchen.

"This was such a good idea!" Carol told Liza a short time later as they both stirred pots of honey on the church stove. "I needed a break from the house."

"I haven't made taffy in ages," another girl said, preparing trays for the candy. "I feel like a kid again."

A small crowd of girls crammed into the basement kitchen, some working on the taffy, others just laughing and catching up. The windows stood open, letting in the warm scent of June sun on the grass. Over the quiet chatter of the girls, Liza heard the snick-snick-snick of the reel mower going over the lawn outside. Her heart caught. George had always mowed the church lawn on Saturdays.

She handed the spoon off to someone else and hurried outside. A familiar figure pushed the mower along. Jack.

Her heart fell. Of course, she had known it wouldn't be George. She felt a flash of annoyance at Jack. When had he taken over George's job? They had been best friends, but that didn't mean he could replace her brother.

"Is that Jack Jensen?" Carol asked.

Liza jumped. A couple of girls had followed her outside and caught her staring at Jack.

She tried to cover her guilty surprise by waving dismissively at Jack. "Oh, yes, it is."

"But I thought he lost his arm," another of the girls said

Liza fought to keep from rolling her eyes. These girls went down to Bushnell with her, but they didn't seem to understand yet what the hospital accomplished. "He did, but that doesn't mean he can't push a mower."

"He must be really strong, then." The girl's eyes brightened. "He was a soldier, too, right? We should ask him to help pull the taffy, then he can tell us if it tastes good enough for Bushnell."

And before Liza could think of a reason to object—or even decide if she wanted to—the other girls flagged Jack down and invited him to abandon his mower for the kitchen. Liza doubted he would. George would have flirted and then gone back to his work, though he would have been happy to steal a taste of the candy when it was done. But Jack left the mower and came over to Liza.

"Making taffy?" he asked.

"For our boys at Bushnell."

He nodded, looking thoughtful. "They'll appreciate that. I'm almost finished. Let me wash up, and I'll help."

Several of the girls giggled in delight. Liza watched him make another pass over the lawn, then he followed her down the stairs to the kitchen. He smiled his way through the crowd to the sink, where he washed his hand and his prosthetic hook. Some of the girls ogled while others looked away uncertainly. Jack didn't seem to notice. He dried up and came back to Liza, standing at attention like she was his general.

"How can I help?" he asked. "I've never made taffy before."

Liza met his eyes, trying to understand what he was thinking. George would have enjoyed the company of all the smiling girls, but he wouldn't have offered to work in the kitchen, especially not taking orders from his little sister.

But, then, Liza was not actually Jack's little sister. She felt a jolt of warmth and a flurry of conflicting emotions about George, Jack, and the whole situation, then put them all aside.

She looked away, her cheeks inexplicably hot. "I'll show you."

Chapter Eight

JACK HAD ALWAYS RESPECTED the magic his mother and sisters performed in the kitchen, but never more so than when he found himself elbow deep in it, trying not to be in the way as girls rushed around with bubbling pots and cooling trays brimming with burning hot sugar goo. In fact, he found the most useful thing about him there was his metal hook, which allowed him to move things that were too hot for the girls to touch.

"It's time to pull it now," Liza told him. She held out a dish of butter.

"What's this for?"

"Keeps it from sticking to your skin." She grabbed a dab and rubbed it into her hands. He watched, thinking how soft her skin looked.

He looked away quickly and scooped up a bit of butter with his hook. He managed to rub it into his rough hand fairly well, and he coated the metal of the hook, too, for good measure.

"You missed a spot," Liza said, and she took his hand, massaging butter into a place he had overlooked. Her touch sent an electric warmth up his arm. It surprised him, but he didn't want her to stop.

This is George's little sister, he reminded himself. He would kill me...

Except, George was gone. That reminder doused cold over him, and he was half-glad when Liza dropped his hand, not meeting his eyes.

This was not the Liza he had known before, anyway. She wasn't silly or tomboyish in the least. She was confident, but with sadness lingering behind her eyes. The war had changed her as it had changed all of them.

And, maybe, Jack hadn't known her as well as he thought.

"We have to stretch the taffy over and over," Liza said quickly. "If not, it ends up hard as a rock."

"That would be a waste of a lot of sugar rations," Jack said with a smile.

Liza laughed, and her whole face lightened. "We can't have that."

They picked up their strand of taffy and pulled it, brought it together, pulled it apart, over and over, as pairs of girls did the same around them. Yet, as he and Liza passed the ends of the taffy back and forth, laughing as they tried to free their hands (and hook) from the sticky stuff, it seemed like it was just them. It felt...comfortable, cozy.

"Did you hear that someone took Mr. Johnston's car for a

joy-ride?" one of the other girls asked, bringing him back into reality.

The young ladies chimed in with the gossip on the incident.

"They found the car abandoned out of gas in downtown Logan."

"Do you think it was one of the POWs? I've heard they've been stealing things."

"I bet one of them took that camera from the store to spy on us."

"I can't believe we let Nazis roam free in our town! This is what you can expect from them."

Jack glanced at Liza. She wasn't saying anything, but an angry crease wrinkled her forehead.

"They don't let the real Nazis come out to the work camps," Jack said, his voice not loud, but cutting through the noise. "Most of those fellows are just soldiers who were forced to fight on the wrong side. Some of them aren't even from Germany—they're Austrians."

An uncomfortable quiet fell in the kitchen. Several girls looked at him in confusion, no doubt wondering why he would defend the Germans. Some of the soldiers hated the Germans, too, and Jack didn't blame them. He had nightmares about the war—sometimes nightmares while he was still awake—but feeling that much anger for anyone just left him exhausted. He couldn't completely put the war behind him, but he didn't want to let it live in his heart any more than he had to.

He glanced at Liza, wondering what she was thinking. Her lips were pressed in a thin line, and her eyes were full of pain. George. Of course, she was thinking of what the Germans had taken from her. It made Jack feel like a traitor for not hating them.

"We should go to a show when we're done," someone finally said in the quiet.

The other girls joined in a chorus of agreement as they chopped their pulled taffy into bite-sized pieces. Liza gave him a curious look as she gathered their strand to cut up.

"What's showing?" someone asked.

"*God is My Co-Pilot.*"

Jack kept himself from grimacing. He wasn't sure a sappy war movie would appeal to him, but he glanced at Liza, and she was nodding.

"Sure," she said. "We just have to wrap up the candy and clean the kitchen."

Jack shrugged to himself and helped the girls finish up. It wouldn't hurt to get out. His mother was always bothering him to be more social, and he could only practice ball with Leroy and his buddies so much before he started to feel like an interloper.

He ran a damp rag over the counter and caught Liza's eye as she gathered the candies.

"I can drive," he offered, "if you need a ride. I used Dad's truck to bring the lawn mower anyway."

She smiled and poured the last of the candies into a tin. "That would be great."

And since they drove together, they—seemingly by accident—ended up sitting next to each other in the plush seats of downtown Logan's Capitol Theater. Jack found himself a little distracted throughout the movie, acutely aware of each time Liza shifted forward during an exciting air battle, her knee brushing his. He decided it wasn't such a bad show after all, even if he couldn't recount many details of the plot.

As the group walked out of the theater into the cool evening air, one of the girls said, "Let's go to the Bluebird for French fries!"

Jack's steps faltered. Liza walked a bit ahead of him, and he closed his eyes for a moment. The last time he had gone to the Bluebird, it had been with George, just before they shipped out. They had laughed about eating there again when they got home. His stomach turned.

"Jack?" Liza asked.

He swallowed. "Uh, I'm not hungry."

"Oh." A vague, stricken look passed over her eyes, and he suspected she understood why.

"I don't want you to miss out," Jack said. "Can you get a ride with someone else?"

She hesitated, and he wondered if she didn't want to eat there either. It might not be bad, he thought, to ride home together with the fresh summer night's wind slipping around them and a quiet understanding between them.

"I can take you home," Carol said to Liza.

Liza looked at Jack for a long moment, then smiled weakly at Carol. "Thanks." She turned back to Jack. "I guess that's all settled, then."

Jack nodded, but he didn't feel settled at all.

Chapter Nine

LIZA COULDN'T STOP THINKING about Jack. About making taffy with him. About sitting beside him at the theater. And she was not thinking of him as George's best friend. She was considering him in a whole new way, and she didn't know what to make of it. She wished she could talk to George about his friend, but she couldn't even imagine what he would say. Would he tease her? Or would he be angry? Especially now that he was gone? He would be proud of her war efforts, she was sure. It was only Jack that confused her. And he was a distraction. She needed to stay focused on winning the war. For George.

In her uncertainty, she packed a small picnic basket and walked east toward the cemetery.

George was buried somewhere in Europe, but their parents had placed a headstone in the Smithfield Cemetery. Liza felt silly visiting it, since George wasn't there in any sense of the word, but sometimes she needed an anchor for her grief. It was too strange at home, where life had to keep moving no matter how they felt. George's room hadn't changed, but Liza kept expecting him to come back to it. At least at the cemetery, she had a reminder that he was never returning home.

She brought a little basket of strawberries from the garden. George had always loved strawberry pie. She wanted to sit and eat the berries and pretend George could hear her as she talked to him about war bonds and Bushnell and the German POWs invading her peace. George had teased her as only an older brother could, but she had been able to talk to him about anything on her mind.

As she walked up the hill to the family plot, she stopped short at seeing Jack sitting next to the headstone. He was leaning against it and looking up at the trees overhead like he had paused in the middle of a conversation. She felt a flash of annoyance, but it vanished when she remembered it must be strange for Jack to be home without George. She hesitated, not sure if she should go, and Jack glanced over and waved to her.

She walked forward, and Jack got to his feet.

"I'm sorry to... to interrupt," she said.

"Don't be. He's your brother."

"He's your best friend."

They both stood there, staring at the headstone with the bleak finality of its dates: 1923-1944. That was it. Those numbers framed the entirety of George's life, yet they said so little about what had made up his twenty-one years.

"You brought his favorite," Jack said, gesturing to the basket.

"Yes. It's silly, isn't it?"

"No. We have to remember."

Liza held out the basket. "Do you want some? I was going to eat them, but I don't mind sharing."

Jack reached for the basket, and his hand brushed hers. A tingle raced up her arm, and she flushed and almost pulled back. Jack paused and wrapped his hand around hers on the handle of the basket. Heat flushed over her face, and she gave him a questioning look.

"You know what's funny?" He asked quietly, a hint of surprised amusement in his voice. "I don't really like strawberries that much. I always thought they had a weird texture. I used to help George sneak them from the berry patch, and I ate them because he did, but I always ended up giving most of mine to him."

He hesitated, then released her hand to take a strawberry and place it on top of the headstone.

Liza smiled weakly. "I like them. We had that in common, George and I." She took a deep breath. "I... I miss him so much. I can't believe he's not coming home."

"I know. I can't imagine it either, and I was..." Jack cut off and looked away, his eyes full of pain.

"You were there?" Liza asked.

Jack nodded, still not looking at her.

She balanced the basket on the headstone next to Jack's offering. "Do you want to talk about it?"

"I don't know. Do you want to hear it?"

She thought about that. Knowing more would make it more real, but maybe she needed that. Maybe it would help her stop looking for him everywhere. "I think I do. The army didn't tell us much. If you don't mind."

He drew a long breath. "It was over fast. I don't think he hurt much. Just, one minute, he was standing next to me, and the next he was down, and there was blood..." He managed to meet Liza's gaze. "He didn't have time to say anything."

Liza nodded, squeezing her eyes shut to stop the tears burning there. "I'm glad he didn't suffer. He was always so... so happy. I didn't like to think of him being miserable at the end."

"No. I think one of the last things he did was joke about how bad breakfast was."

Liza smiled. "That sounds like him."

They stood in silence for several minutes. Liza brushed away the warm tears that escaped down her cheeks. A cool breeze brushed past them, and birds sang in the distance, oblivious to human sorrow. Jack adjusted his prosthetic, staring at it absently.

"So," Liza said quietly, "Yours didn't happen at the same time, then?"

He held up the prosthetic arm. "Nope. A couple of months later. I don't think I was all there, though, after George. I kind of went numb, and I'm not sure my mind was in any of it. It was like I shut down. I suppose I'm lucky all I lost was a hand." He looked up, his gaze vulnerable. "I don't feel like I deserve to get off so easy."

Liza gasped. "But what happened to George wasn't your fault."

"I suppose not. But I still feel... Well, I feel like it's not fair that I'm here and George and all those other men are never coming home."

That bubbling feeling inside of Liza roared to life, and this time, she didn't try to stop it or hold it down. "It's *not* fair! And it's because of the Germans! Hitler and his Nazis. They were greedy and selfish, and they did this to all of us. They're... they're evil. I hate them!"

She broke into sobs. Jack gathered her into his arms and let her cry into his chest, gently stroking her back.

"Hitler's dead, and we captured G-Germany," she stuttered, "But George still isn't back. What's the point of it all?"

Jack just held her until her sobs eased.

"I don't know," Jack finally said. "It's hard to find a meaning to any of it. But I don't think George would want you to hate—"

She pulled away. "Not want me to hate the people who killed him? How can you expect me not to?"

He shrugged. "You have every right to be angry."

"Yes, I do!"

"But the guy who shot him was just another soldier doing what he was ordered. Like George and me."

"No! Don't you dare compare my brother to those monsters! They're all evil! I will always hate them for what they've taken away!"

Liza turned her back on Jack and raced back down the hill, leaving the basket behind. More tears rolled down her cheeks, blinding her, salty when they reached her lips. She furiously rubbed the tears away with her palms. She didn't know if she was more angry or sad or... or scared. Because somehow, the idea of not being angry, of not hating, made her feel lost and confused and like her brother was slipping away from her all over again.

Chapter Ten

JACK DIDN'T KNOW what to make of Liza. He understood why she was angry, but it frustrated him. He felt like they could be friends, like they had a connection that went beyond George, but he couldn't get past the walls she built in his way.

He pitched baseballs—left-handed—against the wall of his family's barn until his dad told him to stop annoying the cows.

He clicked his hook open and closed, then marched out to the fields with the POWs to help thin beets. The POWs took his presence in stride. Most of them didn't know any English, so they mostly ignored him.

The guard gave him an odd look but didn't say anything. He didn't pay much heed anyway. Sometimes, he left his gun leaning against a tree and wandered out of view. Even Jack had been nervous about that at first, but the POWs ignored the gun and worked whether the guard was there or not, probably glad to have something to do to pass the time, and knowing that trying to escape was pointless. If they wanted to take a car for a quick spin or snatch a camera, they probably could, though. Jack had to admit that. He just didn't like how quick everyone was to blame them when they didn't know for certain.

Hans made his way over to where Jack worked.

"It is not much hot," Hans said, glancing at the cloudy sky.

"Not much," Jack agreed. "July will be hotter."

"In *Juli*, maybe is the war over."

"I hope so, but those Japanese aren't giving up." Jack glanced at the man's tired face. "You must want to get home."

"*Ja*," Hans said quietly. "I have fear. My family..." He trailed off and stared toward the east, where somewhere far beyond the mountains, his family was caught in a war, while he was here digging sugar beets.

"Hey," Jack said. "The fighting there is over."

Hans nodded without looking up at Jack, and Jack couldn't blame him. The fighting was done in Germany, but that didn't mean things would be easy there.

Jack's mother came out with drinks for the men, and they all took a break. Jack caught his sister, Rose, watching him among the POWs with a frown on her face.

Jack wondered if there was something wrong with him. If he was still in shock from losing his best friend. He stood aside and watched the German POWs thank his mother for the lemonade. She smiled and responded in English, pretending they weren't speaking her native tongue. He held his prosthetic up and turned it this way and that, noting where the dirt from the field clung to it. He wiped it on his shirt until it shone again.

"How are you doing?" Rose asked, sitting down beside him and offering him a sandwich.

He took it, holding it with both hands—the real one and the metal one. "Do you hate the Germans?"

"That's a heavy question."

"I've been doing some heavy thinking."

She shrugged. "I sure don't like them. Look what they've done to our country. To the world."

He nodded. "I look at those fellows out in the field, and I have trouble connecting their faces with the war."

"I guess it's easier to fight people when you hate them, but it's harder to hate people when you see them face to face."

"Yeah, I think you're right." It was hard to put a face on people you'd fought, too. Hard to think it had been actual people he'd been shooting at. He wasn't ready to talk about that with his sister. Might never be. He and George had ventured on to the topic a little, but it was a dangerous thing to talk about when you had to get up and keep fighting the next day.

He ate his sandwich and watched the Germans. Their guard yawned and stared off into the distance. Maybe he wished he was fighting overseas. Maybe he just wished he was home.

But home wasn't the same when the war invaded everything. Liza's face had looked so sweet as she talked about George, as she blushed when their hands had touched. But there was something frightening in her eyes when she talked about the Germans. The war really was tearing everything apart, whether it was the Germans' fault or not. Jack felt the weight of it, like it was a burden he was supposed to shoulder or to repair. After all, he'd been in the midst of it. He'd survived. Didn't he owe something still, to everyone?

He rested his forehead in his good hand and put his sandwich aside, not sure where his appetite had gone.

His mother's gentle voice caught his attention. She was crouched down, speaking to one of the POWs. Speaking in German. The man sat on the ground, head in hands, his shoulders shaking. Jack had never heard her use German, though he knew she understood it. But now she was comforting one of the POWs.

Rose watched with wide eyes, then exchanged a shocked look with Jack.

Their mother hugged the young man and stood. She hurried back toward Rose and Jack, her cheeks red and her eyes down, like they'd caught her doing something illegal.

"It's difficult to be so far from home," she said. She glanced at the German men, then rushed inside.

Jack's heart felt lighter. At least he wasn't the only one who didn't hate the Germans.

Chapter Eleven

Liza felt guilty for snapping at Jack, but she couldn't push her anger away anymore. She wasn't even entirely sure who or what she was angry at. Jack, the Germans, the Japanese—even George. The emotion had become familiar, almost comfortable. Her frustration boiled over, and now all she could do was put that raging energy to good use. Luckily, the Fourth of July came up quickly—time for the war bond carnival at the church. She had finished the decorations, and she was in charge of the dunking booth. Just as well. She wanted to hit something.

"Here's President Truman's Fourth of July message to the nations," her father said over breakfast that morning, holding up the newspaper.

He read on, but Liza only half listened. She caught the words, "We have confidence that, under Providence, we soon may crush the enemy in the Pacific."

She nodded. Yes, they had to crush their enemies.

When breakfast was over, she washed her plate and hurried over to the church to finish decorating.

"You're here early," said Mrs. Harrison, the president of the local war bond committee.

"We have a lot of work to do!" Liza said, plastering on some fake cheerfulness. She didn't feel any of the real thing, only a restlessness like an itch that couldn't be scratched. "Isn't that what President Truman asked us to do? Crush the Japanese?"

Mrs. Harrison tilted her head. "I suppose he said that. The part I remember best is the ending: 'Freedom is dear to the hearts of all men everywhere. In other lands, others will join us in honoring our declaration that all men are created equal and are endowed with certain inalienable rights—life, liberty, and the pursuit of happiness.' That's why we're doing this, isn't it? So that everyone has the opportunity to be free?"

"Oh, of course," Liza said. But she didn't mean it. She didn't want to see the Germans free. She wanted to see them punished.

She put the final red, white, and blue bows up on the dunking booth. One of them caught her eye—a bow that Jack had made. She smiled and ran her fingers over the curves of the fabric, remembering his jokes about becoming a bow maker. It had been fun working with him, and going to the movies with him. It had made her feel better, for a moment, to talk to him about George. She pulled her hand away from the bow. But wasn't that a betrayal of her brother? Feeling better? Letting go of the anger burning inside of her?

She hurried over to help the other volunteers finish their booths, then returned to the dunking booth. Her first victim was the church's bishop, Bishop Hill, wearing a suit he was willing to have soaked.

He chuckled nervously as he climbed onto the dunking seat. "Here we go. I hope everyone's a bad shot."

"Now, Bishop, it's for a good cause," Liza said.

She checked that her dress was still neat and clean then put on her most inviting smile as their neighbors began to arrive. Women carried treats for the cake walk, made with their sugar rations, and kids ran around the lawn with the tickets they received for every twenty-five cent war stamp they'd purchased.

"Dunking booth!" Liza called. "Who thinks the bishop is all wet? Come and prove it!"

A few of the teenage boys heard her call and wandered her way. Perfect. The more tickets people bought, the more money raised for the war. They couldn't rest until they defeated Japan. Until every American was home. Until Germany had paid for what they did.

Her fake smile, or the allure of seeing the bishop all soggy, seemed to be working, because she quickly had a line at her booth, people trading their tickets for three balls. So far, Bishop Hill had been lucky. The target was harder to hit than it looked.

Then Jack stepped up. He met Liza's eyes and held out his ticket with his hook.

She took it, watching him curiously. Was this his way of donating to the cause? He was a right-handed pitcher without a right hand.

"Jack Jensen is going to dunk the bishop!" someone called.

The crowd gathered, laughing and chattering. They wanted to see the bishop get a dunking, and who better than the former star baseball pitcher to do it? A few people whistled and cheered. Bishop Hill groaned and mimed holding his nose and getting ready to fall.

Then Jack rolled up his sleeves. The crowd grew quiet at the sight of his prosthetic. Maybe they hadn't remembered. Maybe they just hadn't realized until they saw it in person.

Jack held out his left hand, and Liza handed him the first ball. He tossed it up and down a couple of times, testing its heft. He eyed the distance to the target and wound up. Liza held her breath.

The ball flew hard and smacked the booth well off target. A few quiet groans escaped the crowd. Bishop Hill continued to act frightened of falling, but it looked less convincing.

Jack didn't seem disappointed. He took the second ball, once again testing its weight and eyeing the target. The crowd grew still, a few people muttering and others hushing them.

Jack wound up again, narrowed his eyes, and hurled the ball at the target. Again, it slammed into the booth, this time about a foot from its goal.

The crowd groaned audibly now, and little shimmers of whispering spread through them. Jack paid them no heed. Just like he was on the pitcher's mound in high school again. Liza watched him anxiously, silently praying that he would make this last throw.

Once more, he tossed the ball up and down, catching it easily in his left hand. His face remained calm, impassive. The crowd fidgeted. Bishop Hill looked bored. Jack wound up, winked at Liza, and threw the ball.

The ball slammed into the target. Liza gasped. Bishop Hill splashed into the dunk tank and came up drenched and sputtering. The crowds laughed and cheered.

"Jack, Jack, Jack, Jack!"

He grinned at Liza and raised both hands in the air—his whole left hand and his prosthetic right one. Kids whooped and waved their hats in the air. For the first time in days, Liza really smiled.

The dunk booth stayed such a popular attraction after Jack's triumph that Liza was busy taking tickets and handing out baseballs for the rest of the carnival. Only two other guys managed to hit the target, and one young girl who was allowed to stand closer because of her age—though the way she threw, she might not have needed it.

At the end, Liza proudly deposited her tickets into the common pot to show how many people had bought war stamps, then grabbed a lemonade.

"Successful day?" Her mother asked.

"Yes, I think so." She smiled at the crowds enjoying themselves. Jack was heaping a platter with leftover melon. "It looks like Jack worked up an appetite."

"Oh, he's taking it for the POWs at his dad's farm. He thought they should have a treat, too."

Liza set down her lemonade. "The POWs? Why should they? This is a celebration of our freedom. The freedom they were trying to take away!"

Her mother gave her a look. Not angry, but worse. Disappointed. "They've lost their freedom now. Shouldn't we treat them the way we would want to be treated?" Her voice dropped so Liza could barely hear. "The way George should have been treated."

Liza squeezed her eyes shut, her stomach in a jumble of knots.

A local band started playing, jarring against Liza's raw feelings. Some of the other young people joined an impromptu dance on the lawn.

She turned around to find Jack watching her. Her heart fluttered in surprise, but then it continued beating too fast as she met Jack's eyes.

"Hello," he said.

"Hi." She took a deep breath. "I'm sorry I lost my temper the other day."

She glanced over her shoulder and scooted farther from the crowds who might be eavesdropping. Jack walked with her, his eyes sympathetic.

"We're all hurting in some way, aren't we?" Jack asked.

Liza nodded.

"Do you want to dance?"

Liza met his gaze. "You want to dance with George's little sister?"

"No, I want to dance with Liza Ballard."

She smiled a little and took his left hand. He guided her out to an empty patch of grass. He wrapped his right arm around her waist, and the prosthetic prodded her in the side, but it didn't seem so weird, especially since she'd danced with so many men at Bushnell. This was still Jack, but it wasn't the same Jack that she'd known in high school, any more than she was the same Liza. Did that mean Jack liked the Liza she was turning into? Would George have? He didn't fight to punish the Germans. He fought so his family would stay free. Suddenly, she wasn't sure she liked who she was becoming, with anger boiling inside her all the time.

"About the cemetery..."

Jack shook his head. "Maybe, for now, we should just forget everything in the past and enjoy now."

Liza sighed, and a weight seemed to slide off her chest. "Yeah, let's do that."

They danced until the music came to a sudden stop. The bishop, now in a dry suit, stepped up to the microphone.

"Ladies and gentlemen, we have a missing boy. Wayne Vaughn's parents report that they can't find him. He went out this morning on his bike and hasn't been seen all day."

"Oh, no!" Liza said, imagining the poor boy hurt somewhere.

"The police and firefighters will help search soon," the bishop added, "but they've been called to Logan for an accident with some fireworks. We need to start looking now."

The group quickly broke up into search parties, everyone asking questions and speculating about where Wayne might have gone.

"Where was he last seen?" Jack asked a neighbor of the Vaughns.

"Heading toward the sugar beet fields."

"Oh!" Liza whispered.

"What?" Jack asked.

"He's been taunting the Germans. What if he got too close, and one of them hurt him?"

Jack frowned. "We can't rule anything out, but we can't assume anything either."

Liza set her lips in a thin line. "I don't understand why you're so quick to defend them! They've probably killed Americans!"

Jack's face darkened. "Well, I've killed Germans."

Liza paled at the reminder of what he and George and the other American boys had been doing over there. Of what war meant. "That's different," she said quietly.

"No, it's not."

"You protected your country from Nazis!"

"And most of them were protecting their families."

"Ugh! You are impossible!"

Liza stormed off to join one of the search parties. Just as she thought she and Jack had been getting along again. But she could not understand Jack. How could he just forgive people who had caused so much pain and suffering? Who had killed George? If he wasn't angry at the Germans, what was left?

Chapter Twelve

JACK'S SHOULDERS slumped as he watched Liza walk away. It had felt so good—so right—holding her in his arms as they danced, but her anger was going to keep coming between them. He had felt angry for a while, too, but he didn't like how it ate at him. He hated to think of it eating at her, but he couldn't make her let go. He wasn't sure what he could do, except to help look for Wayne Vaughn.

He hurried over to join one of the search groups heading toward the fields where the missing boy had last been seen. They spread out a few feet apart and tromped along the ground, calling Wayne's name and scanning the ground for any sign of him or his bike.

Jack walked on the end of the row, along the irrigation canal. He tripped over something sticking out from the wild roses on the bank of the canal. The handlebars of a bike. His stomach went cold.

"Over here!" he called.

He left the bike where it had been discarded and searched along the canal bank, scanning the murky water below. Had the boy gone swimming alone?

The searchers stared at the bike and then the canal uncertainly, several faces growing pale.

"Search the water," Jack said.

He and several other men scrambled down into the canal. The water was cold and fast-flowing, reaching above Jack's knees. The men walked slowly, some prodding the bottom of the canal with long sticks. Others scoured the brush on either side.

"We might have to shut off the water," one man said. "Just in case."

Jack ran his fingers through his hair and paced, sloshing through the canal water. He climbed back onto the bank, his wet shoes squelching over the dirt. The boy might have left his bike for another reason. Maybe he'd gone up into the mountains. He glanced down at the men working in the fields. Or maybe Liza was right, and Wayne had gone to confront the Germans. They should have been under strict watch, but their guards were often not very alert.

Jack recognized one of the work details below. They were often assigned to his father's fields. He had trouble imagining any of them hurting a child, but he didn't actually know them.

"Keep looking," Jack said to the other searchers. "I'll be right back."

He jogged down to the fields.

The guard stepped into his way. "Where are you going? No socializing with the prisoners."

Jack held up both arms, and the guard's eyes fell on his prosthetic, softening his expression a little.

"We're searching for a missing boy," Jack said. "Any chance he could have come this way?"

"No one's allowed to socialize with the prisoners."

"And you were watching the whole time?" Jack asked, raising an eyebrow. "We found his bike right up there by the canal. You must have seen something."

The guard sighed. "Okay, it's possible he sneaked past. I was on the other side of the field for a while, taking a break, and the local kids always want to get a look at the 'Nazis.' They don't get that these aren't the bad ones. These guys just want to earn their eighty cents for the camp canteen and get home."

"I know," Jack said. "Can I ask if they've seen anything?"

"You speak German?"

Jack shook his head.

"Me neither. All I know is what's on these cards." He showed Jack an instruction card with agricultural terms in English and German.

"Well, unless the kid decided to play hooky to thin beets, that's not going to help much." Jack handed the card back.

Some of the Germans had noticed the commotion on the hillside and stopped working to watch. They turned interested gazes on Jack and the guard as they walked over.

"Any of you men seen a little boy?" the guard asked, speaking very loudly and slowly.

The Germans looked at each other. A couple shrugged.

Jack gestured to show a child's height, and he pointed to

his eyes. "Seen a child?" What was the word the man had used when he saw Gladys? *"Kind? Bitte?"*

A couple of the Germans whispered to each other. A few shuffled their feet and kept their eyes down. Jack's stomach sank. They knew something.

Jack approached them. "You've seen?" he asked, pointing to his eyes.

One man pointed to the mountainside. *"Vielleicht. Da."*

Jack looked back at the guard, who shrugged. "They're always daydreaming about those mountains. Guess it reminds them of home. They could have been watching up there."

Jack hesitated. He knew the Germans were holding something back. Something that might help him find Wayne. He scanned the faces again, and he spotted Hans making a very deliberate effort not to meet his eyes. His heart sank. He knew they weren't friends, but he'd felt a connection with the German mechanic.

He wandered closer to Hans and whispered, "You have seen?"

Hans shook his head and said loudly, *"Nein. Ich weiss nicht."* In a lower voice, he added, "I see. A boy yell with a soldier. He run."

Jack's pulse picked up. Had Wayne argued with one of the guards? Was that what the prisoners were afraid to say? "Your soldier? This one?"

"Nein. Another," Hans whispered. Then, he pointed to the mountains and said in a louder voice, *"Vielleicht da."*

Jack stood debating. One of the other guards nearby might know what had happened to Wayne. But if the man had chased Wayne off, he might not want to admit it. The mountains seemed like their best chance of finding the boy. Jack and George had explored the canyons often as boys.

"*Danke!*" Jack called to the Germans, remembering one of the few words he'd picked up at Bushnell. "Thanks!" he told the guard. "Keep your eyes open, in case, right?"

The guard nodded.

Jack raced back to the other searchers.

"The prisoners think they saw a boy heading into the mountains," Jack said. "We should head up the canyons to search."

The other men shifted and exchanged skeptical glances.

"Why don't we pass that on to the firefighters and keep searching along the canal?" one man asked.

Jack glared at him. "Because we're here now."

"It's getting dark," another man said. "We don't even know if those Germans were telling the truth. They might be sending us on a wild goose chase. Trying to get us lost or hurt."

"Or distracting us from finding the boy," someone added.

Jack squinted into the gathering gloom. The long shadows made it difficult to see in the brush, but he'd done plenty of night missions in Europe. "There are black bears in the mountain, and the river's running high and cold after all the rain we've gotten. I'm not taking the chance of leaving that kid out there alone." He looked back at the other men. "Some of you can stay here to keep searching the canal. The rest of us head up there. We stay together, watch each other's back, and we keep looking until we bring him home."

Jack stared the men down, daring them to back out.

George would have stayed with him, but he would go alone if he had to.

"Okay, we keep searching," one of the men said, and the others nodded.

Jack divided the men into two groups, taking some of the younger ones up into the canyon with him. They pressed on through the gathering darkness. The moon peered over the ridge, casting a bright glow over the junipers and scrubby maples.

"Wayne!" the men called, their voices disrupting the stillness of the mountainside.

From time to time, Jack caught a glimpse of the lights in the town below. Could Wayne see them, too? If so, the boy would probably try to make his way back down. The danger was if he was stuck somewhere and he couldn't see anything to guide him.

"Follow the creek," Jack suggested. He and George had hiked up there plenty of times, and there were lots of little gullies and ridges where someone could get hurt or lost.

The men kept calling as they hiked, though their voices sounded less sure than before.

"Wait!" one of the men yelled. "I thought I heard something."

The men stood in the moonlight, listening. An owl drifted overhead. Then Jack heard it, too: a faint call for help.

"That way!"

The search party tromped through the sage and brambles, calling with renewed vigor.

"I'm over here!" the boy's voice came much more clearly. "Help!"

Jack scrambled over a rise and found Wayne propped against a boulder, his leg twisted at an odd angle.

"I've got him!" Jack called. "Looks like a broken leg."

"I fell," Wayne said weakly.

"I know. It's all right."

"I... I had to run away. I saw one of the guards take something from the house. He spotted me and said we could just blame the Germans. But it wasn't right. He was stealing. I was afraid he was going to shoot me. So I ran."

"Oh, kid, I'm sorry. Most of them are decent men, but there are a few bad apples."

"I thought we were the good guys."

"Sometimes things aren't that simple. Sometimes the people who should be good guys do bad things, and the people you thought were bad guys aren't so bad after all."

Wayne lowered his head.

Jack considered how to lift the boy out without hurting him more. He was glad now that the other men had come with him. He had seen the way stretcher bearers on the battlefield carried wounded men, so he had some idea how they could get the boy back down the rough terrain.

"I'm going to lift him up to you," Jack said to the other men. "Two of you need to grab him by the arms and pull him up. Try not to jostle his leg." Jack turned back to Wayne. "We're going to do our best not to hurt you, but you need to be brave."

Wayne nodded, his face pale in the moonlight. "I'm just glad you found me."

"Thank the Germans," Jack said as he maneuvered

himself down to get a good grip on Wayne. "They saw you heading this way."

"Oh," Wayne said.

Anything else the boy might have wanted to ask was cut off by the necessity of Jack climbing down and getting back-to-back with Wayne. He linked his arms with the boys' and hefted him up high enough for the other men to grab the boy and lift him out of the crevice. Jack climbed up after them. Two of the men linked their arms together to form a sort of chair for Wayne. Jack and the fourth man guided them back down the steep trail.

As they walked, a warm satisfaction settled over Jack. He had done it. He was afraid that everything good he might have done had been left behind on the battlefield, that he didn't really deserve to make it back when so many others hadn't, or that his missing arm made him unable to really be good at anything. Yet he had helped rescue Wayne. For the first time since leaving Bushnell, he felt like he could see a future for himself.

Chapter Thirteen

LIZA PACED IN THE KITCHEN, too upset even to find something to keep her hands busy. They had searched around town until it grew dark, and there was still no sign of Wayne Vaughn. Liza didn't know what else she could do. Her dad turned the radio on in the other room, listening to some mystery program, and Liza wanted to cover her ears against the distraction.

The phone rang. Liza gasped and spun around, but her mother had answered it before she could.

"I see. Thank you for letting us know," her mother said. She hung up the phone. "They found Wayne Vaughn."

"Found him?" Liza clutched her hands. "Is he—"

"He's alive. Apparently, he caught one of the guards stealing from a house while everyone was at the carnival. The guard threatened Wayne, and he ran off. Wayne fell and broke his leg up in the canyon. Some of the German workers saw which way he went and tipped off the searchers."

"Oh." Liza sat heavily and stared at the jars waiting to be washed. "One of the guards was the thief?"

"Yes. Some of the POWs knew, but they were afraid to speak up. Wayne identified the man, and he'll be court-martialed."

Liza put her head in her hands. "I'm so glad Wayne is safe." She looked up. "And the Germans helped find him?"

Her mother sat in the chair next to her. "Yes. They're not all bad, you know."

"They killed George!" The old fire kindled inside of her, but now, it made her feel tired. Like she'd been burned and hollowed out inside, and she just wanted to rest.

Her mother sighed. "I suppose some Germans somewhere did, yes. But I don't think of it that way. I think it's this terrible war and the evil in the world that killed him."

"But you can't fight all the evil in the world." Liza's mouth felt numb at those words. Wasn't that what she was trying to do?

"No, we can't. All we can do is try to make our little corner of the world better. We have to leave the rest in God's hands."

"But He doesn't fix everything! He lets all these horrible things happen."

"Yes. He lets people choose. Sometimes, I wish he didn't. But freedom is obviously very important to God, too. I just trust Him to make it all right in the end. Somehow." Her mother's eyes filled with tears.

Liza looked away. "I feel like I'm betraying George if I stop fighting." She clenched her chilly hands in her lap.

Her mother laid warm fingers over her fists. "George

would always want you to stand up for what's right, but he would also want you to be happy. He was always happy. And I don't think you can be happy if you hold on to your anger and hate."

Liza lowered her head. Hot tears streamed down her cheeks. She slowly pulled away from her mother's touch and walked down the hall to her room. She paused on the way to peek into George's room. She knew her mother was right. George would tell her not to stay angry. To find a reason to laugh again.

"I don't know how," she whispered into the dark.

There was no one to answer her.

Liza remained in a daze. Her anger gave way to a gaping emptiness, and she went through the motions of her days without feeling anything except the weight of weariness. When Sunday came around, she didn't want to face church. She didn't want to be around other people. She didn't want to listen to lessons about peace or forgiveness. And she especially didn't want to see Jack or think about the things she had said to him.

She dressed automatically, out of habit, and followed her parents down the road to the church house. During the meeting, she kept her eyes down, and the words of the sermons buzzed around her head without finding a place to land.

As soon as it was over, she hurried outside, standing apart from everyone. She was tempted to scan the crowd for Jack, but she didn't know what she would say to him. She ought to apologize for snapping at him—again—but he probably didn't want to talk to her anyway.

Members of the congregation gathered in gossipy knots, but Liza leaned against a tree and stared off toward the mountains in the east. Beyond them, somewhere, lay George. By now, grass would be growing over his grave. She hoped it was a lovely and peaceful place for him to rest.

Liza's mother walked over and gave her a tight squeeze.

"What was that for?" Liza asked.

"I'm just so glad you're safe. The world is so uncertain, and after hearing about what happened to those Germans—"

"What?" Liza asked.

"You haven't heard?" Her mother's forehead wrinkled in worry. "Down in central Utah. Salina. There was a guard at a POW work camp like ours who shot his machine gun into tents full of sleeping German prisoners."

"What?" Liza's skin went cold. "Why?"

"All he would say is that he hated Germans and wanted to shoot at some."

"Did he... Are they..."

"Several are dead, many more wounded. They're bringing some of the injured to Bushnell."

"We're not at war with Germany anymore," Liza said, and the words struck her.

"Hate and anger don't stop with a surrender."

Liza covered her mouth, tasting bile. She walked home, trying to make sense of the news. A camp full of sleeping men injured and killed. They and their families must have thought they were safe, just waiting to return home and try to rebuild their lives. They were attacked, not because of what they'd done. Just because a guard hated what they were.

Just as Liza did.

This was not who she wanted to be. It's not who George would have wanted her to be, either.

She was up most of the night worrying about it. What could she do? She couldn't get rid of all the anger and hate in the world, but, as her mother had said, she could start with her own corner of the world. With herself. She wanted to pluck those feelings out of her chest and plant something new there.

"I want to do something for the Germans here," she told her mother the next morning. "They'll hear the news about the shooting, and I'm sure they'll be upset."

"That's thoughtful of you, but we're not allowed to socialize with them."

"But Jack's mother brings them lunch." Liza perked up. "That's what we'll do. We'll bring them a picnic. Show them that we're not their enemies, either."

Her mother's eyes shone with tears. "I think that's a beautiful idea."

Now, Liza was on solid ground again. She knew how to organize. She got on the phone and went to work recruiting her neighbors. Her family had a little extra from their garden. Almost everyone had a little extra. They could bring it all together to make something big.

They gathered in the church kitchen with a bit of flour or sugar here, a few tomatoes or squash there, and by lunchtime, they had a feast of roasted vegetables, salads, and quick biscuits.

"Perfect," Liza said, inspecting the dishes they'd created. "Now, we take it to the POWs for their lunch." A few of the women looked a little regretful to give up what they'd created, so Liza added, "They've had some bad news. They're probably scared and homesick. It's what we would want people to do for our boys overseas."

The women nodded and carried their plates and baskets away. Liza joined the group going to the Jensen farm. She owed him an apology.

The guard hurried over when he saw them approaching. "What are you ladies doing?"

"We're bringing the prisoners a picnic," Liza said.

The guard looked confused. "You can't socialize with them. No fraternization."

"But we can leave it for them, can't we?" Liza asked. "For their lunch?"

The guard scratched his head. "Well, I suppose you can."

The women spread out the baskets of food and stepped back. The guard called the dusty prisoners over. They stared in surprise at all the food. The baffled Germans yelled, "*Danke!*" and waved excitedly as they dug into the baskets.

Jack's family stood on their porch, watching the POW picnic and talking with the guard. By the serious looks on their faces, Liza guessed they were talking about the shooting and not the picnic.

Liza looked away. Maybe the picnic was a silly idea. It wouldn't actually help the men attacked in Salina or their families. Just like her efforts at Bushnell and the war bond drives would never bring George back. The picnic had made

84

these men happy for a few minutes, though, and it made her feel less helpless.

"This was your idea?" Jack asked, suddenly close by her side.

Liza spun to face him, and her face warmed at an awareness of his closeness. "It was. I thought they might be upset, and I wanted them to know... to know that we're not all like that guard."

"I think this is a good idea. George would be proud."

Liza flushed. "And what about you?"

"I'm proud, too," he said, and stroked back one of her errant curls.

Liza shook her head. "I haven't done much lately to be proud of. You went out there and saved Wayne, and you knew where to look because you believed the Germans."

"I feel like I need to give back. I came home, and George and so many other fellows didn't. I guess I was kind of angry at myself. You were angry at someone else. It's natural to be angry, but we can't move forward until we let go of it."

"It almost feels wrong to move forward," Liza said.

"I know. But that's what I realized up there on the mountainside, looking for Wayne: if we owe anything to George and the others, it's to keep going forward. We do whatever our part is to help bring this war to an end, and then we keep living. For us and for them."

"You think so?" It felt like a burden lifting from Liza's shoulders.

"I know it's what George would have wanted. He would have wanted us to be happy." He cleared his throat. "I know everything's different now. But do you think we could move forward? Be happy? You and I, I mean."

Liza met his eyes. "It is different now... and, yes, I think I'd like to try."

Jack grinned and held out his hand. Liza hesitated, then took it. Jack smiled and guided her back a few steps, so a lilac bush gave them a semblance of privacy. Liza turned her hand to lace her fingers with Jack's. He stroked the back of her hand with his thumb, sending a pleasant shiver up her spine. He released her hand and touched her face gently, then leaned down to kiss her. She lost herself in the soft feeling of his lips on hers.

"So, that's where you snuck off to!" Jack's sister Rose said in triumph.

Liza quickly broke away from Jack, her face burning. Her mother was there, a smile on her face.

"George always wondered why you two never seemed to notice each other," her mother said. "I guess you were just waiting for the right time."

"I guess so, ma'am," Jack said. He stood at attention, a faint blush coloring his cheeks, too.

She wagged a finger at them. "But no more sneaking off behind the lilac bushes, you hear me?"

"Yes, ma'am," Jack said with a grin.

He held out a hand for Liza. She took it a little shakily, and together they walked back to the farmhouse.

Author's Note

This story is loosely based on events that occurred in Utah during WWII. Bushnell General Military Hospital in Brigham City was the main military hospital for the West Coast, and a primary recovery center for amputee soldiers, sailors, and marines. Important advancements in wound treatment and prosthetics came out of the efforts to help the patients, such as the plier-like hook (or set of hooks) that Jack wore—a tool that was strong enough to lift every day objects but delicate enough to tie shoes and fasten buttons.

Famous Utah saxophonist Joe McQueen and his band really played at Bushnell's dances for free to support the war effort (and perhaps because the hospital was one of the few unsegregated institutions in Utah at the time), and the Idle Isle offered free meals to amputee soldiers who could walk through the restaurant doors. Though most of the Bushnell Hospital buildings have since deteriorated and been removed (after serving for many decades as Intermountain Indian School), you can still eat at the Idle Isle Cafe today.

The Logan Fairgrounds were home to one of many POW work camps in Utah. The camp's location in the heart of town was controversial, but the farms needed the POW labor until the local men returned from the war. The scene with the homesick POW crying over the sight of a local child is based on an actual event, as is the tension between the German and Austrian prisoners. The thefts and the incident with Wayne Vaughn are my inventions, but the presence of the Germans and Austrians in town caused a lot of worry, and some of the American guards were also considered troublemakers.

The shooting at the Salina, Utah POW camp, sometimes called the Midnight Massacre, occurred in the early hours of Sunday July 8, 1945. One of the guards fired a machine gun into the tents of sleeping German and Italian prisoners of war, killing nine men and wounding nineteen others. He said he did it because he hated Germans and wanted to shoot some. He was declared mentally unfit and institutionalized. The victims were buried in the Fort Douglas Cemetery in Salt Lake City, and there is now a museum at the site of the Salina Work Camp.

Though I invented the picnic for the Logan POWs, many Utahns were horrified and outraged by the shooting. Those who had POWs working on their farms often befriended the POWs despite the language barrier and the rules against fraternization, and some maintained those friendships even after the POWs returned home.

Also by E.B. Wheeler

British Fiction:

Born to Treason

The Royalist's Daughter

The Haunting of Springett Hall

Wishwood (Westwood Gothic)

Moon Hollow (Westwood Gothic)

A Proper Dragon (Dragons of Mayfair 1)

An Elusive Dragon (Dragons of Mayfair 2)

A Subtle Dragon (Dragons of Mayfair 3)

Cruel Magic (Irons & Thorns 1)

Utah Fiction:

No Peace with the Dawn (with Jeffery Bateman)

Letters from the Homefront

Balm of the Heart

Bootleggers and Basil (in *The Pathways to the Heart*)

Blood in a Dry Town (Tenny Mateo Mystery)

The Bone Map

Nonfiction:

Utah Women: Pioneers, Poets & Politicians

Mysteries of the Old West

Acknowledgments

A shorter version of this story originally appeared in the Cache Valley Authors collection *In the Valley*. Thank you to everyone who helped with that original version and with this one, including my critique group The Writers Cache, authors Jeff Bateman, Emily Daniels, Janeal Falor, Lorin Grace, and A.M. Luzzader, and beta readers Karen Brooksby and Laura Sharp. And my gratitude and love, as always, to my family, who make it all possible.

About the Author

E.B. Wheeler attended BYU, majoring in history with an English minor, and earned graduate degrees in history and landscape architecture from Utah State University. She's the award-winning author of over a dozen books, including *No Peace with the Dawn*, *Letters from the Homefront*, and *Utah Women: Pioneers, Poets & Politicians*, as well as several short stories, magazine articles, and scripts for educational software programs. In addition to writing, she sometimes consults about historic preservation and teaches history, and she enjoys gardening, fiber arts, folk music, and exploring the West with her family.

You can find more about her and her books at ebwheeler.com

www.ingramcontent.com/pod-product-compliance
Lightning Source LLC
Chambersburg PA
CBHW071955230626
47052CB00014B/1154